A DODO'S LIFE

A Sourdough Mystery

Suzanne Parrott

A Dodo's Life, *A Sourdough Mystery*
Cozy Mystery with Wit, Wisdom and Bifocals
by Suzanne Parrott
Created in collaboration with Anja Elen & Maren Sage

Parrott Publications

First Edition September 2025
ISBN: 978-1-960350-08-4 (hbk)
          978-1-960350-06-0 (pbk)

Cover Illustration: "Walter's Dodo Life," Suzanne Parrott, Anja Elen
Cover Design, Interior Layout: SuzanneFyhrieParrott.com

*You can read monthly author interviews, enter contests for prizes,
read published stories, join discussions and be offered a chance
to read unpublished stories. Please visit:*
DodoDiaries.com

To Mandy —
For every laugh, every tear,
every moment we share.

———

Dodo Diaries

A Dodo's Life,
A Sourdough Mystery

A Dodo Detective
(coming 2026)

A Note from the Author

My name is Walter, and I have a dodo's life.

Life gets called boring sometimes. But boring, in my experience, is just quiet joy wearing its house slippers.

This book holds only a few entries. Some long. Some short. Several barely a thought, and some wandering around looking for reading glasses.

I've always been a writer. Odd notes about life written through years of perception. Memories, now more feeling than factual, that carried hopes for the future and from my final twilight years.

I started writing again after Clara passed away. Bits and pieces of a life, scattered like breadcrumbs.

You'll find a few dodos within these pages. The kind you don't notice going extinct until one day they're gone. Paper maps. Rotary phones. The sound of a typewriter. A particular cologne your father wore. Or a real person answering the phone when you call the bank.

Quiet moments that shape us, then slip out the back door unnoticed, forgotten.

Life is filled with things that remind us where we've been, what we loved, and how we came to be who we are.

And, sometimes, life is filled with mystery. Like how one anonymous note (or three) can shift the weight of your day. I didn't know what I was chasing. I only knew something was waiting to be found. And I've always liked the finding part.

So, my friend, if you find within my musings something familiar or perhaps nearly forgotten—then I've succeeded.

May your life be filled with Dodos.

Walter

P.S. My life was filled with Clara. Still is.

My Dearest Clara. I miss you.

Forty-Two Years of Rooflines

There was a time when routine suited me. Predictable days, scheduled naps, toast the same shade every morning. But somewhere along the way, comfort turned to crust. I wouldn't have said I was bored—but routine had grabbed hold like an overzealous octopus and wouldn't let go.

Fortunately, change was already halfway up the driveway.

We purchased the house with a fixed-rate mortgage and a leaky sink, both were long-term commitments. The sink was patched (the first time) within the year. The mortgage took a little longer.

Still remember the day Clara and I pulled up—her holding the realtor's flyer, me pretending I wasn't worried about the roofline.

The porch sagged.

The garden all weeds.

The kitchen smelled like old onions and vinegar.

Clara walked in and opened every window. "It has bones," she said. "And heart, if we stay long enough."

We did.

The house has shifted over the years, like my waist and

hairline. A new porch, new paint, a few too many ceramic gnomes in the flowerbeds (her doing, not mine.)

Mow the lawn with the same gas-powered mower we bought the first summer.

It's louder now.

So am I.

Fair enough.

There's a chair in the living room that Clara sinks into like a sigh. I sit by the window and watch the neighbors forget their garbage days. We've had our share of noise, our share of silence.

It's mostly quiet now. That works.

I don't know what people expect after four decades in the same place. Excitement? Renovations? We've had both.

But mostly we've had *days*. Good. Some difficult. And enough ordinary days to make this home a part of us.

Clara still weeds the garden. I still check the roofline.

And in the morning, we sit on the front porch with our coffee and nod at the world like we've seen it before— and like it just fine.

Pancakes Again

Leanne, our daughter, moved away the same summer the azaleas finally bloomed right. A job offer in a city that buzzed even at night—too far, too fast.

Clara cried on the way back from the airport. I didn't. I stared and drove slower.

We supported her decision, of course. That's the job of parents: launch and hope. And we did hope—hoped she'd be happy, safe, busy, loved. She always was a bit of a comet. Full of life, moving fast, hard to hold.

Three years later, she called.

Pregnant.

I nodded as if I saw it coming.

I hadn't.

Clara started knitting before the call ended.

Jason, our grandson, arrived five years ago, and every photo filtered through joy and chaos. Bright-eyed, loud laugh, covered in peanut butter half the time.

Last year, she moved back. Said the noise of the city never settled in her bones, and the school system wasn't what she hoped for, and maybe—just maybe—being closer to her parents wouldn't be such a bad idea after all.

We let her make her own choices.

Always have. Right or wrong.

This was right.

Felt it in the way Clara filled the kitchen with pancakes again. In the way the boy—our boy—ran through the sprinkler in the backyard like he'd lived here forever. In the way Leanne looked, as if it was the first time she'd breathed in years.

She lives ten minutes away. Drops in with Jason after school sometimes. Leaves socks on our couch and yogurt in our fridge. I step on toy cars occasionally and don't even complain. Much.

Some returns don't need a reason.

Just an open door and pancakes.

The Internet Box

I didn't trust it. Arrived in a box inside another box, which already felt excessive.

Clara called it a modem. I called it a blinking menace.

When we had dial-up, at least you knew when it was working. It sang a little robotic opera: whines, beeps, one long screaming hiss.

You'd pour your coffee and know, "Ah. It's connecting."

Now it sits there. Silent. A panther in the cupboard.

Clara says it's faster. I say it's lurking.

She set it up in five minutes. I stared at the instructions as if written in ancient Sumerian.

I offered to hold the screwdriver.

She didn't need one.

It has lights on the front.

Sometimes they blink, sometimes they don't. I asked Clara what that meant.

"It's working."

That's no answer. Fireflies blink. Doesn't mean they're up to anything good.

Last night I asked it what it wanted. Clara said it couldn't hear me, but I don't believe that. If it can send cat videos across the globe, it probably understands sarcasm.

I cover it with a dish towel at night. Just in case.

Staring Contest

The microwave isn't a microwave anymore. It's also a clock. A bad one.

If the power flickers—just once—off it goes, incessantly staring: "0:00."

Like the countdown had ended. But to what?

At least the VCR has the annoying decency to blink. Every living room in the country had one.

"12:00. 12:00. 12:00."

Like a silent chant.

Some technologies assume they are more intelligent than their owners. I blindfolded the VCR with black electrical tape.

Problem solved.

Now the microwave has taken up the torch. Clara says I should just reset it. But the buttons are small, and my fingers are not.

Tried three times.

Set the timer and cooked an invisible meal.

Finally set it correctly. (I thought.) Was two hours and sixteen minutes fast. Lived a whole afternoon in the future.

We have three clocks in the house.

None work properly.

The old wind-up clock on the mantel doesn't tick anymore. I still glance at it like it might start working again.

I know what time it is.
The clocks know too. They're just being stubborn.
Or planning a coup.

Magenta Demands

Tried to print a chicken recipe today. One page. Black and white. Clicked the little icon like usual. The printer responded by growling and then asking—no, demanding—new magenta.

Magenta.

The recipe is black and white. There is no magenta chicken. No raspberry-glazed poultry. But the printer insists it cannot possibly print anything until it has been sufficiently magenta'd.

Pulled out all the cartridges from the drawer like a dentist checking molars. Shook them. They appeared full. Certainly enough to produce one ink-starved chicken breast.

But no magenta.

Clara says we'll order more. I say this is a hostage negotiation. The printer holds all the power. Somehow, it knows to demand the one color we don't have.

Back in my day, if your pen ran out, you dipped it again. If your ribbon wore down, you thumped it and hoped for the best. Now the machine gives you attitude. "Cannot proceed without magenta." I can't proceed without dinner, but you don't see me throwing a tantrum.

I wrote the recipe out by hand.

Printer's still sulking.

So am I.

The Notebook

Clara says I shouldn't write down passwords. It defeats the purpose.

Remembering seventeen different combinations of uppercase letters, special symbols, and the maiden name of a goldfish I never owned *also* defeats the purpose.

So I keep a notebook. A small one. Tucked in the junk drawer between the mostly-dead batteries and a screwdriver with no handle. The book is labeled "Birthday List," which is accurate and misleading.

Each password has a little code next to it.

Netflix is "Binge Box."

Bank account is "Old money."

Email is "Where the junk lives."

Clara caught me updating my list. "You'll lose that book one day and someone will get everything."

I said, "If they're brave enough to go in that drawer, they deserve it."

She rolled her eyes, but smiled. That's compromise.

I get to keep my notebook.

Went shopping yesterday. Forgot the password to the grocery app *and* the notebook. Called my daughter. Was instructed to "Just reset it."

Thinking of changing all my passwords to: "IHateNewThings123!"

Three Pulls and Earplugs

Spent the morning with the car. Just routine—checked the oil, topped off the washer fluid, kicked the tires like I knew something.

Not a classic, just old. Early '90s. Paint's faded; there's a spot over the wheel well that's thinking about becoming a hole.

Still, she starts, she turns, and she doesn't talk back.

I like that in a machine.

Modern cars don't trust you. They beep, flash, and refuse to unlock if your phone isn't in your pocket.

My car trusts me. Needs me. That's a relationship.

Same goes for my lawnmower. I call it the mini-car.

It's red—or used to be. Pull cord's touchy, and it backfires if you look at it wrong, but we get along fine. I understand its moods.

Three pulls if it's cold. Two pulls if I prime it right. One pull if I whisper nice things to it the night before.

Neighbor came by while I was fiddling with the mower blade. Said he'd bought one that mows itself. Plots its own route. Uses an app.

He asked if I wanted help.

No, thank you. This one and I have an understanding.

Clara laughs when I come in with grease on my hands like I'd been in a prize fight. Said I looked happy.

I was.

It's comforting—machines that you can hear, touch *and* fix. Not everything has to plug into the wall or come with an instruction video narrated by someone named Bryce.

Sometimes, all you need is a good wrench and a little patience.

And earplugs.

That mower is loud.

Out With the Old

Clara bought new silverware today. Said she needed a change. The others were old and tired.

The new ones are sleek, no frills, unpretentious.

I held up the old spoon in my hand.

Welcome to the club, I thought.

Hid the old set in my shop.

Hope I'm not next.

Sleek and the Silver Skunk

Tried to watch the TV while Clara was out with "the girls."

Found three black remotes on the coffee table. One tall and sleek, one with a faded silver stripe up its back, like a skunk, and one unimpressive, like a thin black brick.

Tall and Sleek: Pushed a button. The lamp turned off.

Pushed a few more. The stereo turned on, playing something called "lo-fi beats." I didn't ask for lo-fi beats. I don't even know what it is.

Clara used to keep a Post-it under the TV remote with instructions. I assume it was for me, as she never looked at it.

Today, the note is missing. Either the cat got it or the house swallowed it, like it does with reading glasses and socks.

Silver Skunk: Press a button, heard a whirring noise. It didn't sound happy.

Unimpressive. Pressed the red button. TV turned on, but it was a menu. Asked me to update the firmware. I declined. I don't know what firmware is, and I've never updated it. I don't trust things that ask for permission to become something else.

Turned everything off. Read the newspaper. No batteries. No firmware. No lo-fi anything.

TV can wait.

Clara will be home soon.

Galvanized Memory

We went to the hardware store today. Clara needed something for the curtain rod, and I never turn down a reason to visit a place that smells like lumber and possibility.

She headed to the home aisle. I drifted toward the screws. There's something deeply satisfying about those tiny drawers—brass, zinc, galvanized. No one needs this many types of fasteners. But I like that they exist.

Found a man in the paint section staring at color cards like they were quantum mechanics equations. Said he needed "something bold but not regrettable."

I wished him luck.

Clara found me near the caulk. Held up her package like a trophy. We checked out.

She asked if I wanted to stop for coffee. I said yes before she finished the sentence.

Sat by the window. Clara stirred her drink like she was composing music. Outside, a kid decided to lick a lamppost. He looked surprised it was cold.

I smiled.

Went home and watched "A Christmas Story."

George

We went to the nursery today. Clara said we were just "looking." That's code for coming home with at least three things and a new gardening project I didn't know I wanted.

Store smelled like potting soil and damp roots. Reminds me of childhood—digging in the backyard, looking for treasure, finding worms.

Clara found the herbs. I stayed by the ferns. One looked like it needed a friend. A little sun-scorched, leaning a bit left.

I liked it.

Does anyone still garden? Not flowerbeds designed by landscapers. I'm talking about dirt under your nails, crawling on your knees gardens. Where plants grow even if you forget to water it once (or twice.)

Clara placed the fern in our cart. "You two seem to understand each other."

We did.

We also brought home lemon balm and oregano. Clara already named the fern George. I'm not sure it's a George, but I've been wrong before.

The Last Scone

Clara took a nap today.

Not common, but when she does, the whole house joins in. Even the cat stopped trying to open the cupboard, curled up in the laundry basket, and blinked slower than usual.

I stayed in my chair. Didn't move. Much. If you're too loud during a Clara nap, she gives one of those silent looks—where her eyebrows put you on report.

She naps with a book open. "Just resting my eyes," she says. But the bookmark never moves. Sometimes I wonder if she selects boring books as sleeping pills.

Silence is thicker when she's asleep. As if the house is holding its breath, waiting for her to awaken and say, "You didn't eat the last scone, did you?"

I didn't. Not today.

But I hid it. Just in case she wanted it later. That's love, I think. Not a grand gesture—just saving the last scone so someone else can pretend they didn't want it.

Ducks with Tenure

Went to the park. The little one. Clara likes the benches—says they don't make them like that anymore.

The ducks have unionized. Waddle over the moment you sit down, like you've interrupted a board meeting. Now you owe them bread.

We didn't bring any.

Clara scolded me like I'd forgotten an anniversary.

She walked ahead on the path for a while, arms swinging carefree like she did in her twenties. Like time is something she can negotiate.

I trailed behind, watching, thinking how the park feels the same as when we first met. The same cracked fountain, same squirrels, probably. They've got tenure.

A kite rose into the sky on the far side of the field. Not fancy—a diamond of red with two wooden sticks.

Probably store-bought. Looked homemade.

The kind you'd spend hours building from a kit and then promptly lose the same afternoon.

Kids used to do things by hand.

Another dodo. Soon to be a forgotten footnote in a future history book no one will read.

I took Clara's hand. She smiled. Didn't say anything.

Sometimes, silence is better than talking.

Easier on the ducks, too.

The Kite

When I was ten—still trick or treating, but wise enough to know everything—I built a kite.

Used a large sheet of butcher paper; found two mismatched sticks from Dad's garage and a bottle of glue.

The park—the big one downtown, with the statue of the man pointing off toward the freeway—was holding a contest. I don't remember the prize.

Billy (my best friend since birth) dared me to enter. Said I couldn't build a kite that could fly straight. I said I could make a kite that could hit *him*.

Worked on it for three afternoons. Took over the kitchen table. Mother kept moving it to set dinner. I had string in the butter and sawdust in the salt.

Mother never complained. Not that I know of. I suppose she was just happy I was doing something constructive.

When done, I had glue in my hair, my clothes, and places best not mentioned.

But I had a kite. Sleek. Simple. Mine.

The day of the contest. It flew. Not well. Not high. But long enough to catch the wind.

It felt great.

Didn't win anything, of course. The winner had a kite shaped like a shark with spinning fins and a tail that whistled.

Show-off.

But I remember running across the grass, heart thumping, shouting at the sky. The string biting my fingers. The paper flapping like it was trying to break free.

Perhaps, I'll make one again. See if I remember how.

For Jason.

I'll need help with the glue, though.

Reunion

Clara's 55th high school reunion was this weekend. I've now attended five of them—six if you count the year I got the date wrong and showed up to a quilting conference by mistake.

I enjoy *her* reunions. It's like time travel, but with punch and name tags.

They used to be big evening affairs. Now, they're in the daytime, with less dancing and more chairs. I don't mind forgetting names anymore. Just wave, smile, and say, "You look great," which is reunion-speak for "We made it."

Clara glows at these events. Laughs more, stands taller. Says it's nice to be remembered for something other than grocery lists and dental checkups.

I agree.

Overheard someone say she hadn't changed. I didn't correct them. I quietly admired how her silver hair matched her earrings and how she still tucks her napkin in the same tidy fold.

Billy was wearing a shirt covered in tiny boats. He only comes to every other reunion. Says that "statistically, the best snacks happen on the odds." He's got a system.

He created "pop-up reunions" whenever he travels. Apparently met someone from the Class of '68 at a bait shop in Omaha, Nebraska.

Now they exchange handwritten postcards.

Snail mail.

Slower, but more heart. More memories.

After all, the tortoise won the race.

At one point, the DJ—a polite man with a tablet—asked for couples married over 50 years to stand. I nudged Clara's arm.

She said, "Close enough," and stood.

We danced. Slowly, carefully. Mostly in place. She said I still lead too much. I told her she still hums the tune in my ear.

We got a round of applause. I think it was for staying upright, but still—it felt good.

Zoned for Love

Dearest Clara,

I've been reminiscing about the first time we met.

It was when they rezoned the school districts, the dividing line ran straight down the middle of our two-block street like someone splitting a sandwich. Billy went left. I went right.

Although Billy was sent to a *rival* high school, we stayed best friends. Couldn't help it. He lived across the street.

I didn't mind. It was how I met you.

You sat behind Billy in English, apparently corrected his grammar once, and scarred him for life.

He complained about it for a week. You sounded terrifying.

Then one Saturday, I saw you at one of Billy's game nights. You wore a plaid skirt and sensible shoes, as if you were leading a field trip.

I asked if you liked board games.

You replied, "Depends. Do you cheat?"

I immediately fell in love.

We ended up on the same team for charades. You acted out *Wuthering Heights* with more gusto than should be legal in a basement rec room.

I sat there mesmerized. Then blurted, "Catherine?"
You smiled.
At me.
As if the entire stormy moor was mine.

Billy rolled his eyes. "Good guess, Heathcliff."
But it wasn't a guess. It was you.

That was the start.
The rezoning never mattered after that.
Because, it gave me you.

Love, Walter

Plumbing

Decided to fix the bathroom faucet. Announced it like I was embarking on a sea voyage.

"Good luck, Captain," Clara replied.

For weeks, I'd avoided the problem. It was the cold knob. It would stick a little, and then pop open like a floodgate. Needed tightening.

But when I opened the cabinet, it was like looking at the underworld.

Pipes. Damp wood. One very judgmental spider.

Gave it a wiggle. (The faucet, not the spider.) Then gave it a firm turn. The handle came off like a souvenir.

Clara came in to check on my progress. Lied and said it was going fine.

She glanced at the knob sitting on the counter like miniature gravestone. "I'll get a towel."

Put the faucet back together, mostly. No leaks. Although the cold tap rotates in both directions and cries like an offended goose.

I told Clara it added character.

She added a plumber to the to-do list.

And placed a new towel under the sink, just in case.

The Game

Billy picked me up for the boys' soccer game. Our grandsons are on the same after-school team—the "Lightning Bolts."

Sounds fast.

False advertising.

Clara stayed home to do "laundry." That's code for wanting quiet time. She's good at knowing when to let men grunt and holler.

Tossed my underwear into the laundry basket, just in case.

Arrived early. Staked out our spot on the metal bleachers with a blanket Clara insisted I take and old thermoses filled with hot coffee.

"You'll freeze your kidneys," she warned. Not sure which organ is in charge of bleacher temperature regulation, but I took the blanket anyway.

The park looked the same—patchy grass, a lone tree trying to shade the snack shack, and a field lined with orange cones.

The ref was about 14 years old and all knees, voice still cracking. He blew the starting whistle like it owed him money.

Within seconds, two dozen six-year-olds ran off in every direction. My grandson, Jason, was the goalie, wearing oversized gear that swallowed him whole. Stood with arms wide, knees bent, legs bouncing as if preparing for lift-off.

Billy's grandson was all legs and enthusiasm, charging after the ball like a bullfighter, then suddenly started swatting the air as he ran off the field.

"A bug," Billy said.

One of the opponents came barreling down the field and fell mid-sprint, pants sagged just enough to reveal a full plumber's greeting. The boy didn't blink. Popped up off the ground and kept running.

That's commitment. I've experienced and offered the plumber's emblem many times in my youth. Now, it happens without warning.

Went out for cocoa after the game. Billy spilled his across the counter while trying to open a packet of sugar. Blamed his gloves. I blamed his birth year.

Back home, Clara met me at the door with warm, folded towels and a smirk. "Well? Did you behave?"

"Nope," I said, holding up a sticky cocoa-stained glove.

She rolled her eyes.

She missed me.

Red Checker Blues

Dearest Clara,

I found a red checker under the radiator. No idea where it came from. My heart tightened, as I held the small wooden piece—bringing me back to that day at the hospital.

You always said hospitals need more than doctors—they need kindness, coupled with sensible shoes.

It was a Tuesday. You wore your cardigan and carried a look that said someone is going to feel noticed today.

"Just sit with someone who needs company," you said, like it was a simple thing. I grumbled, of course. Always did. Said I didn't like hospitals, that I'd get lost or accidentally join a surgery team.

You rolled your eyes, clipped a visitor badge onto my shirt, and kissed my cheek like you knew I'd survive.

They paired me with a boy, seven or eight. Sharp as a tack and missing most of his hair. He looked at me like I was the entertainment.

"You know how to play checkers?" he asked.

"Badly," I said. The boy grinned and set up the board.

We played every Tuesday and Thursday. Was beaten thirteen times in a row.

I won the last game—probably a goodwill gesture to keep my ego alive.

He had a book of knock-knock jokes, none good, but he told them as if new material.

Called me "Old Man Wally" and insisted I salute when he'd captured my king.

I called him "Your highness."

The third week, I entered his room and the bed was made. The board game gone. No chart on the door.

I didn't ask. Was afraid to.

You found me standing in the hallway, hands in my pockets, staring at the floor as if the speckled tiles would erase the emptiness. You didn't say anything. Stood beside me, shoulder to shoulder, like you always did when I was too quiet to reach.

I sat on the edge of the couch, holding the red checker like it belonged to him. Maybe it did. Maybe it was left for me to find.

A small piece of wood with so much memory attached.

I gently tucked it in the top drawer. Not the junk one. The good one.

Clara, you always knew when someone needed to be seen. I'm still learning.

Love, Walter

Nothing Day

Today started with the perfect chair hug.

You know what I mean—coffee in hand, seat cushion like it remembered you from yesterday. A little warm from the sun, soft, supportive, and happy to see you.

Clara padded into the room in a pink robe and with that soft shuffle I'd recognize in a stadium full of slippers. Gave me that morning smile, the one that's still half asleep, but still lights up my heart.

We settled in—each with our own book, our own mug, our own silence.

She dozed off twice. Her head dipped, then popped back up as if nothing happened. Still, the most beautiful woman I know.

Clara never drools. Not once.

I, on the other hand . . .

The sun filtering through the window, spotlighted hundreds of tiny dust dancers that lazily floated about the room. Even the cat sprawled belly-up on the rug, quiet and non-judgmental (for once.)

I didn't fix anything. Didn't clean, didn't organize, didn't even finish the crossword.

Yet, somehow, the house felt happier. *I felt happier.*

As if the world took a quiet breath for the day.

It was perfect.

Note from Walter

Some days, we enjoyed a quiet life, and those are the ones I miss most. I may not remember every errand or argument. I will remember the light on her face when she laughed at nothing.

This day was like that—just two people in a house, doing absolutely nothing.

In Your Face Grandson

Clara said my phone was ringing. I couldn't hear it. Was in another room.

Used to be that incoming calls echoed down the hall, up the block, and across state lines if need be.

Now the phone just lights up and waits.

No yelling, no notice.

It was Jason.

FaceTime.

I still find it unnerving and intrusive. There's no grace period—just your surprised face staring back. No time to adjust your hair or put on dignity.

Jason grinned. Two front teeth missing.

I said he looked like a hockey player who'd kissed a frozen puck.

He said, "Cool."

We talked about his soccer game, his science project (a volcano that burped dish soap and red dye), and how he wants to invent a drone that feeds pets. I told him to add a feature that folds laundry and makes toast. He frowned, confused.

Clara waved from the couch. He waved back, then showed us the cat. Not their cat. Just . . . a cat. Apparently, it visits sometimes. I asked if it had a name.

He said, "Yeah, but it changes depending on the day."
Then waved and hung up.
Felt rude. Shouldn't there be a bow?
Clara said, "He has your grin."
He has your stare, I thought. "Poor Kid."
She smiled, and gave my cheek a peck.
Sometimes, it's best to remain silent.

Southbound

Looked in the mirror this morning, and noticed something was off. Not in the normal way—I'm used to that face by now. But something had shifted. Took me a moment to find it.

The part in my hair has migrated.

It used to be a neat, off-center country road. Now it's drifting south, like a retiree with a beach condo in mind. It's making a beeline toward my ear. If trends continue, it'll bypass my earlobe and settle somewhere on my chin.

I asked Clara if she'd noticed.

"Oh sweetheart, I stopped trying to find your part years ago."

Comforting.

I'm grateful I have hair. Billy's been combing his eyebrows over the top for over a decade. I'm not brave enough to be bald—too many oddly shaped heads in my family tree.

Nothing I can do. Let the part wander. Maybe it's searching for purpose, like the rest of us.

The Neighbor

New neighbor moved in today. The old Colby place.

Young guy. Skinny jeans. Shoes, no socks. Hair appears to have been styled with a whisk.

He backed a dusty green hatchback up the driveway.

I waved from our porch.

He gave a quick nod in response—like we were part of the same gang.

Carried in two suitcases, a lamp with no shade, and a milk crate of books. No mattress, no furniture. Through the window I saw him set up the books on the kitchen counter. Must be using it for a desk.

Clara scolded, said not to spy.

"Neighborhood Watch Patrol," I said.

She scowled.

I pretended to stare at the bushes, while making mental notes.

The next day, we brought over a plate of welcome cookies—oatmeal raisin, the diplomatic treat. Friendly without being forward. I stood beside Clara like a potted plant.

"Just moved in?" she asked.

"Yesterday," he said, glancing at me.

"Well, we're next door if you need anything," Clara said. "I'm Clara. This is Walter."

He nodded again. "Nice to meet you. I'm Ben."

That was it. No last name. No explanation. No hint of where he came from or why he moved into a house that's been empty since the Colby boys moved their mother to assisted living five years ago.

Later, I saw him in the backyard. No lawn chair, just sitting cross-legged in the grass with a book and a mug. Like a monk.

Clara thinks he's a writer. I think he's planning a heist.

Something about him seems . . . familiar. Can't put my finger on it. Maybe it's the way he looked at the tree by the fence. Or the porch swing.

Or me.

Anyway. We've got a neighbor again.

Let the window watching commence.

Mystery Letter

Clara asked if I'd checked the mail. I had not.

I don't check it every day. Mostly coupons, bills we paid online, and invitations to buy burial plots "before it's too late."

Tempting.

Today was different.

A letter. Unsealed. No return address. Handwritten, in blocky print like someone trying not to be recognized.

Inside: an old, folded piece of stationery stock that smelled faintly of dust and cinnamon. Could've been my mailbox, or my imagination. Or Clara's cookies from last week.

Not new paper. Thick, soft, yellowed around the edges.

The note just said:

"She called him 'O.B.' You should know why."

That's it. No signature.

I asked Clara, "Did you call anyone 'O.B.'?"

She paused. Then shrugged. "Maybe. A long time ago."

She didn't seem concerned. Went right back to folding laundry. But I noticed she folded the towel three times instead of two.

I stood in the kitchen, holding the note. Tucked it in

the back of the junk drawer, behind the rubber bands and spare keys.

Could be a prank.

Might check the Colby house. Just walk by, see if our new neighbor gets strange mail too.

If I get caught snooping, I'll say I dropped a coupon.

Not the worst lie I've told.

A Note from Walter

I didn't know it then, but this was the start. Just a small envelope, no stamp, a few block letters. Mysteries don't start with flashing lights. They slip in quietly, like most important things do.

Smells Like Paper

Clara weeded the front flower bed. I cleaned the litter box. The cat supervised. Scooped kitty candy bars and nuggets with one hand while holding the mystery note in the other.

Someone stuck it in my mailbox by hand. That's illegal, technically. But so is mailing a coconut without packaging, and I've seen that done too.

"Do you know who O.B. is?" I asked the cat.

He blinked, turned, and used the litter box I'd just cleaned. That's a no.

The envelope followed me all morning. Through breakfast, half a crossword, and the laundry, which I only started because Clara said we're down to our "Tuesday towels," which aren't fit for guests or even us, really.

Got the mail. And another note. Same M.O. Folded. Plain white. No return address. No stamp. No envelope. (Guess he ran out, or trying to save money.)

Same Blocky handwriting. Not Clara's. Not mine. No one I know. The note said:

"I've been wanting to thank you — O.B."

I held it up, squinting, hoping it might reveal a secret code. Nothing. I sniffed it. (Don't ask why. I think I was hoping for lilacs. It smelled like note.)

Could be someone from church. Could be one of Clara's friends. Could be a neighbor. Could be a mistake.

It *is* the start of a mystery.

So I made a list of possible places to look:

- Clara's Yearbook (in the closet for reasons known only to her)
- Address Book
- Library
- Billy
- Google "O.B." (prepare for disappointment)

Also added:

- Buy cat food
- Return Larry's shovel (again)
- New pen (this one skips like a nervous rabbit)

I've been circling that envelope like a dog with a new smell on the rug. Part of me thinks it's nothing. Part of me wants to know everything.

Life doesn't hand you many puzzles after 70. Most of mine are printed in the back of the newspaper and come with answers.

This one—I'll let it simmer.

Circling the Mystery
(and the Casserole Table)

Sunday, which means church. The building hasn't changed since I was a boy, except the hymn numbers are now projected on a screen and the coffee's gotten weaker.

Half-listened to the sermon. Something about letting go of worry. Or maybe it was about wheat. Hard to say. I was preoccupied.

O.B.

Scanned the backs of heads during the second hymn, trying to recall anyone with those letters. Olivia B. from the choir? She's about 12. Possible chain letter. Doubt it.

Possibly the man who sings like a sad accordion. Or the woman who brings her parrot on Wednesdays. (That bird could have written it. He says thank you and knows four curse words.)

Shuffled into the fellowship hall after the service. Same beige linoleum, same folding tables. Usual food lineup: unknown casseroles, low-cal cookies, and a punch flavored with hand soap and nostalgia.

Took two cookies, one safe-looking casserole, and one deviled egg. It stared at me sideways.) Made a slow circle of the room. Not mingling—circulating. Clara calls it my "vulture lap." I call it recon.

No one slipped a note in my pocket. The only disturbance was from a horrified teenage boy exclaiming his muffin had raisins.

Horrors of horrors.

Clara sat across the room, laughing with her friend Diane. Head thrown back, eyes sparkling. A woman who chooses to keep joy close.

I like it when she laughs like that. Makes the whole room feel warmer, even when the church A/C is set to Arctic Chill.

She caught me watching her. Gave me a look—curious, affectionate, slightly amused. Like she knows I'm up to something but won't ask—yet.

I folded the O.B. note back into my pocket.

Tomorrow, I'll start with the yearbook.

For now, I'll let the mystery sit next to me, just out of reach, while I finish my coffee and eat the second cookie I swore I wouldn't.

Oatmeal, Blueberries and Aqua Net

Monday. Cloudy. Just enough chill to justify the wool socks again. I call it "early cardigan season." Clara calls it "still August."

Breakfast was oatmeal. Plain. No sugar, no cinnamon, no fanfare. Just oats doing what oats do best—being beige and dependable.

Clara placed a small bowl of fresh blueberries beside me without a word. She does that—adds color to my life. Blueberries and all.

She sat with her tea and asked, "So how's your mystery coming along, Mr. Detective?"

I shrugged. "Probably someone from high school," I mumbled between bites. "Initials O.B. Could be Olivia... or maybe Oliver... or Orville?" I paused. "Or maybe Ostrich Bennigan, the silent exchange student."

Clara smirked. "Ostrich moved to Denmark after senior year. Married a pastry chef."

After rummaging in the hall closet, and a small thump (possibly the board game shelf rebelling), she returned holding her Jefferson High School yearbook—senior year.

Placed it on the counter like it was evidence.

"Here you go, Watson. Start with the usual suspects."

I opened the book and immediately smelled my own adolescence. Ink, dust, and a slight tinge of teenage desperation. So many hairstyles. So much Aqua Net. It was like flipping through a zoo of earnest creatures who didn't know they would someday become extinct.

Clara finished her tea while I paged slowly. "Are you hoping for a smoking gun in there?"

"No. Just a mildly smoldering clue." I'd even settle for moldy.

She kissed the top of my head and carried our bowls to the sink. The yearbook stayed behind. So did the blueberries. I'll finish them later. For now, I have suspects to review. And apparently, a partner.

She's the Holmes to my Watson.

Or the blueberries are.

Either way, I'm on the case.

Sourdough Secrets

Tuesday afternoon.

Clara and Diane left for their hair appointments with the usual swirl of perfume and plans. Appointment marked with a post-it on an old 2008 calendar of mountains.

Calendars repeat every seven years. Clara knew that. Which meant the same kittens—or ducks, or Italian villas, or roses, or mountains, or an aerobic sloth (don't ask)—cycled back through like an old bus route. Reliable, but a little predictable.

I like variety. One year I printed pictures off the internet—castles, lighthouses, even a submarine—and taped them over the kittens. Clara was not amused.

I was.

I had just settled into the quiet, made tea, and cleared the kitchen table—meaning I shifted everything slightly left—when there was a knock at the door.

It was the new neighbor. He held a brown paper bag and looked as certain as a man holding a live chicken. "I have something for Clara," he said. "Oh, and you too."

I nodded, stepping aside.

He glanced at his watch. It was one of those sleek devices that simultaneously monitors your heartbeat, stock portfolio, and alibi.

"I only have a few minutes," he said.

"Long enough for tea?"

Ben hesitated. Then nodded once. He didn't say much, which was fine by me. The cat sniffed his shoes and immediately lost interest. Always a decent judge of character—though he once adored the mailman, who routinely folded our newspaper like it had insulted his mother.

The man placed the paper bag on the table. "Sourdough," he said. I opened it and gave it a look. The real kind. Dense, crusty, the smell just right.

He smiled politely. "I bake when I can't sleep."

Homemade. I cut off the end; the crunch and flavor filled the air.

Real bread. The kind with integrity.

"Clara tried making sourdough once," I said. "Twice, technically. The second effort was an attempt to erase the memory of the first. Starter smelled like something the cat dragged in, buried, then reconsidered."

He laughed. Eyes sparkled. Not much else. Wasn't sure if it was shyness or conserving words like battery power.

We sat in the kitchen with mismatched mugs—mine chipped, his borrowed—and the bread between us like a peace offering.

"Ever consider opening a bakery?"

Another smile, this time slower. "Maybe, someday."

His watch buzzed, and lit up like a runway.

"Appointment," he said, standing.

Of course. Everyone has one.

"Thanks for the bread," I said. "And the mystery."

He looked at me, confused. I gestured to the O.B. letter, still tucked under the edge of the cookbook like a bookmark for a recipe I hadn't decided on yet.

"Odd note showed up in the mailbox the other day," I added. "No stamp. Just initials."

He said nothing, shook his head with eyebrows raised. His watch buzzed again. Gathering his things, he gave a parting nod, and left with the same quietness he arrived with.

I stood at the sink, chewing. Thinking. Should have asked for a handwriting sample.

The mystery stayed with me. The initials. The timing.

O.B.

Oatmeal and Blueberries.

Other Boyfriend.

Oven-Baked.

It meant something.

And the neighborly sourdough bread?

Well. That meant something, too.

Clara walked in ten minutes later with wind-kissed

cheeks and a new haircut that she said made her feel "feathered." I told her she looked like spring.

She sniffed the air. "You used the oven?"

"Not guilty. Neighbor."

She paused. "He came inside?"

"For tea. Said he bakes when he can't sleep."

"Ah. Wise man."

She took a slice without asking, buttered it without looking, and kissed my shoulder on the way out.

I added "bakery" to my list of possibilities.

- Clara's Yearbook - no O.B.
- Address Book
- Library
- Billy
- Old calendars
- Diane
- Bakery

And now:

- Watch the neighbor.

Carefully. Just in case he's more than a man with flour on his hands.

Calendar Day

A detective needs a sharp eye, steady nerves, and, in my case, a hat covered in hair.

The closet is the cat's "special place." It's warm, or perhaps it's another way to annoy me. (Not that he needs help.) The creature climbs onto the shelf, naps in my cap, and leaves me wearing evidence.

Clara said no true investigator looks credible with whiskers stuck to his head.

No choice. It's the only hat I own.

Rummaged through the closet for Clara's calendar box.

Why would anyone need to know what day March 14, 2009 fell on? We all have quirks. Mine involves buying more pens when I already have plenty. Clara's was time travel via the hall closet.

Dragging the box to the kitchen, I flipped through the kitten calendar whose images were thinner, happier, and less opinionated than ours. Bygone days filled with Clara's perfect cursive handwriting—appointments, meals, birthdays, and cryptic notes like "green shoelaces," or "Remind Walter: goats."

Then I saw it.

O.B.

Written in red pen on a Tuesday. Circled. Nothing

else. My heart lurched. I sat down on a storage tub of winter sweaters and stared at the entry.

Could it be someone Clara had known? A secret? A visitor? An alias?

Obstetrician? A baby?

Oh Lord!

Not Clara. Couldn't be.

I'd read in the Bible about Abraham's wife, Sarah. Wasn't she 90? Miracles had priority.

I could see the headline:

Local Woman, 70, Stuns Science.
Husband faints. Cat Unimpressed.

I flip back a few pages. Leanne's baby shower. Cupcake order.

"Ask Walter: cradle."

Right. That baby. Our grandson.

My heart starts beating again.

O.B. "Order Balloons" or "Orange Bib."

I tucked the calendar back in the box, sat there a minute more, then went out and swept the porch like a man who hadn't just aged ten years in three minutes.

Mystery can wait.

Even detectives take breaks.

Mrs. Everly's Library

Donned my detective hat and took the cat for a walk today. He used to act insulted by the baby pack carrier, all mesh and straps and indignity. Now he tolerates it. I think it's because he can hiss at squirrels from an elevated position. Power changes a man.

We did our usual loop—down Maple, around the duck pond (no ducks today, just a kid throwing bread at the water and narrating his own pirate adventure), then up to the old library.

They tried to tear it down once. Developers wanted to put in something shiny and modern—"live-work condos," which, to me, sounds like an apartment that makes you answer emails at dinner.

Thankfully, someone had the good sense to declare the building historic. Now it stands, slightly crooked, with brick the color of old toast and a door that sticks in the summer.

Inside, it smells like paper and lemon polish. The whole place is quiet in the way churches try to be but rarely succeed.

Mrs. Everly still runs the desk. She must be eighty by now. White bun, wool cardigan, eyes like a birdwatcher's—sharp and amused. She once caught a teenager trying to sneak a phone call in the corner and made him read *The Old Man and the Sea* out loud as penance.

He still sends her Christmas cards.

"Walter," she said as I entered, cat strapped to my chest like a marsupial with opinions. "What brings you and your familiar to the stacks?"

I asked if she remembered anyone with the initials O.B. She paused, finger to her chin.

"Living or dead."

"Either."

She tapped a pencil on her notepad. "Well, there was Oscar Beasley. Taught music. Liked socks with cartoon instruments on them. But he moved to Arizona years ago."

No bell. Nothing.

"Well, there was Otis Bledsoe," she said. "Used to deliver eggs in an old white van with a painting of a rooster on the side. He died several years ago."

Still no spark.

She peered at me for several moments, the pencil now tapping against her lips. "Perhaps you're chasing a ghost."

"Maybe. Or a memory."

Mrs. Everly smiled and handed me a flyer for next week's community book sale. "Keep chasing. We need more people around here with interesting hobbies."

Then the cat sneezed. Loudly. And I felt something warm and wet seeping into my shirt.

We made our exit.

O.B. Still unknown.

But now I've got a deceased egg man, a music teacher, and a community book sale on my calendar.

And laundry. Need a new shirt.

Progress, apparently.

Oscar Wilde in the Third

Rain today. The polite kind, not the sideways sort that slaps you for being outdoors.

I packed the cat in the carrier anyway. He gave me a look that said, *"Really?"* but didn't protest. We made it as far as the end of the driveway before he did a slow-motion pivot in the mesh pod and sat with his backend in my face.

Fair enough. I grabbed the mail and returned to the house. Bills. Catalogs. And . . . another note.

Again, folded once, and tucked square in the mailbox like it belonged there.

This one had my name on it. Same blocky printing. Every letter widely spaced as if they were afraid of each other.

Clara swears she didn't see anyone drop it off, and went right back to buttering her toast like we weren't living in a spy novel. That woman could be calm during an alien invasion. "Perhaps you've got a secret admirer, dear," she said and winked.

This note didn't say much more than the first. Just a quote.

"Memory is the diary we all carry about with us."
– Oscar Wilde

I don't carry a diary. Clara says I barely carry my wallet. No explanation. No "O.B."

I was about to toss it in the drawer when I noticed something—down in the lower corner, faint as a ghost's sigh.

A watermark.

I squinted at it with the magnifier I keep in the junk drawer. Held it up to the window. The letters shimmered just enough to catch the eye.

Penmark & Co.

Not a brand I recognized. Sounded fancy. Like paper for lawyers or poets.

"You could check the paper shop downtown. They used to carry brands like that." Clara said as she walked by with her coffee.

I looked up. "Didn't that place close two years ago?"

She smiled, took a sip, and nodded, "Exactly."

Three notes now. A quote. And a paper trail.

I tucked the evidence beside the others and added "Penmark & Co." to my list.

Figs & Crowbars

Friday. I couldn't possibly go out again today—not without raising Clara's eyebrows so high they'd need a permit. The cat was already eyeing me like I was about to start packing for Peru. Three outings in a week? Scandalous.

The creature perched on the windowsill like a gargoyle all morning, as if to say *Don't even think about it.*

And I wasn't. I'd decided to let the paper trail rest, sort the drawer of cables we probably no longer needed, but kept just in case.

Then Clara, sweet savior of curiosity, glanced up from her recipe book and said, "I could use a few fresh figs for dinner. The little grocery store past Brenner's might have them."

Figs! I tried to play it cool.

"I suppose I could go. Get some air."

"Don't get lost," she said without looking up, which may have been a joke or a subtle warning. Hard to tell. She's got a twinkle that plays both ways.

So off I went on a noble fig quest. Definitely *not* to case a closed office supply store with a crowbar.

The cat watched me go with eyes narrowed.

Gave him a quick nod as if saying: I'll let you know what I find.

He yawned.

Criticism noted.

Undercover work can be exhaustive.

As I reached the corner, I glanced back at the house.

The cat sat in the windowsill, watching me, tail twitching.

If he'd had a notebook, he would've written:

Subject left residence,
suspicious behavior,
probable return with fruit.

Closed for Business

Brenner's Office Goods. Could this be who I am looking for? I chuckled. I'm looking for O.B., not B.O.

The store smelled of dust, ink, and that odd tang of dried-out tape. Not a lively place—unless you're an accountant, a pen snob, or someone on a paper trail.

Michael Brenner stood behind the counter, sorting legal pads as if first editions. Recognized him from church; good tenor voice, likes lemon bars, never misses a bake sale.

The rest of the shop—dust on the staplers, a thin film on the display case—business wasn't good.

"Walter! This is a surprise."

I gave my best business nod. "Thought you were closed."

He nodded. "What can I do for you?"

"I'm looking for paper."

He smirked, clearly curious if I'd taken up calligraphy or origami.

"We are a supplier to larger businesses, but I may have some loose stock in the back. What do you need it for?"

I took the note from my pocket and laid it on the counter as Exhibit A. "Any chance you've seen this brand?"

Michael leaned over, adjusted his glasses, and gave a thoughtful hmm. He picked up the page as if it was a delicate fossil.

"Well now . . . Haven't seen this in a while."

The watermark was a local stationery brand that stopped production in the 1950s. "Old stock," he said, tapping the corner. "We used to supply it to law offices—real traditional types. The hospital too. Had a huge back stock. But the last sold over two years ago."

He handed back the note. "Sorry."

Hospital. My brain filed that in bold print.

"Not many people request this anymore," he added. "But I might have a box or two buried in the storeroom, if you're interested."

I wasn't. Not really. But I nodded anyway. Man on a mission. And I could always use more paper.

Michael didn't ask what the note was about, which made me like him more. He simply said, "Good luck," the way someone might say to someone building a boat in the backyard.

I said thank you and left with a box of paper in one hand and a breadcrumb in the other.

Glancing back, I frowned at the Closed sign tucked in the corner of the dusty front window.

The trail was getting warmer . . .

and more confusing.

When I walked into the house, Clara looked at the box, then at me. "More paper?"

I shrugged. "Evidence." She raised an eyebrow.

"Careful, Watson. Don't lose the plot."

Cargo Shorts Philosopher

Friday night. Reviewed the list again. Not the grocery one—though that did lead me to figs and paper detectives—the *mystery* list. I keep it in the back of the same spiral notebook I use to track trash pickup days. Clara thinks it's grocery coupons. She'd be surprised to learn how much espionage lives under a Buy-One-Get-One-Free for green beans.

I looked at the items:

- Clara's Yearbook – no O.B.
- Address book – mostly dentists and dead people
- Library – more dead people, donate books, wash shirt
- Old calendars – scare of a lifetime
- Billy
- Google "O.B." – nothing
- Hospital
- Penmark & Co. – bought paper from closed shop (ghost?)

I doubted Billy would have any insights into the mysterious letters.

So, if the paper came from the hospital . . . maybe the person did too.

I circled *Hospital* twice, then added *Monday* in the

margin. Clara would be off with her girls' group, so I could poke around without interruption.

Not that she's nosy—just terribly efficient at piecing things together. She knows I'm up to something. Worse—she's enjoying it.

But first: Saturday.

Another soccer game. Grandsons wearing helmets and kneepads like miniature knights, charging across the field with reckless abandon and very little ball control. We claimed our usual spot on the metal bleachers, both armed with travel mugs and peanut snacks.

The coach taught them to pass, which meant half the game was spent with the boys yelling each other's names at high volume, and the other half consisted of random pileups near the sidelines.

"You think your grandson knows which goal is his today?" Billy asked, squinting.

I shrugged. "As long as he keeps his pants up, I'll call it a win."

He laughed and elbowed me. "Remember that kid last week?"

"Oh, the Plumber's Apprentice? Legendary."

We cheered as our team scored. The player raised both

arms in triumph, then tripped over his shoelaces. A solid 10 for enthusiasm. Billy stood to clap. I stayed seated; I'd just found a comfortable spot. These old knees don't like do-overs.

Clara arrived armed with orange slices and drinks like a one-woman U.S.O. operation for sweaty grade-school soldiers. Stationed by the folding table near the sideline, she doled out snacks with military precision. Caught her laughing with one of the players who'd lost a shoe at halftime.

The game ended in a knot of high-fives and spilled water bottles. Billy and I stood and wandered toward the snack table, where our boys, red-faced and proud, devoured orange slices like they'd won the World Cup.

"You ever notice how some people can drift back into your life?" Billy said, handing me a juice box like we were twelve again. "Maybe life's trying to finish a thought it started."

I laughed and shook my head. Billy gets philosophical once in a while, usually in cargo shorts.

Still, I wrote his comment down when I got home.

Familiar Territory

Church was uneventful in the best kind of way. Don't remember the sermon, again—something about vineyards and patience. The pews creaked and the music held a warm familiarity.

Clara's hand found mine halfway through the final hymn. She wore the blue sweater I like, the one that smells of cedar and dryer sheets. We didn't talk on the way home. It felt like a conversation all the same.

After lunch, I sat on the porch with the newspaper. Clara had dozed off inside, her book in her lap.

I've been chasing ghosts all week. Not sure if they lead somewhere or are just playing tag.

Time to thank Ben for the bread.

Found him in the garage sanding an old chair and covered in sawdust, like a woodshop snowman.

"That sourdough didn't last a day," I said "Clara already put in a formal request for more."

He grinned, wiped his hands on a rag and gestured for me to follow him into the house. "Glad to hear it. She dropped off a casserole dish earlier—smelled too good to be legal."

He offered me another slice of fresh baked sourdough, still warm. We stood in the kitchen, chewing in companionable silence. Then I followed him to the living room.

His house was tidy. A couple moving boxes stacked in the corner. A folding chair and TV. On the mantle sat a silver-framed photo—white room, balloons, and a small boy with a bandaged arm.

Something familiar. I scrutinized the boy's crooked smile that created a dimple on his left cheek.

My heart fluttered.

Sweet, yet sad.

Gazed at the image for several moments. Then, finished my bread, thanked him, and walked back across the street.

With the boy in the photo, following me.

Elementary, Dear Watson

Clara left early to meet Diane for tea. "Don't wait up," she said with a wink, "We have pastries to criticize."

She wore my green scarf. The one she claims isn't mine, despite all evidence, and scarf law, to the contrary.

Waited until the house was quiet. Grabbed the car keys and informed the cat I wouldn't be long. He gave me the look reserved for deep betrayals—like leaving the house without treats.

Rushed to the garage. The old car engine coughed like a man waking from a nap.

As I started to back out, I saw Ben driving away.

What *is* his last name? I eyed the mailbox across the street in my rearview mirror. Hands fidgeted on the steering wheel.

I could go check. Looked down the street to the left, then to the right. Glanced at the mailbox again. I shook my head, backed out slowly, and headed in the same direction as Ben.

The drive to the hospital was shorter than I remembered. Funny thing about memory—it stretches out the things that hurt and compresses everything else.

Parked in the far corner of the lot. No reason. Just habit. I sat for several moments, the cooling engine ticking in the silence. The windows began to fog.

Some memories don't knock. They wait quietly, then slap you upside the head.

The boy.

A hospital room.

Playing checkers.

Laughter that cracked through the antiseptic silence.

He'd been so sick. And then . . . gone.

The memory made my heart ache. I almost backed out right then—unsure if I was still chasing ghosts.

Then I saw him.

Ben.

Walking through the glass doors of the hospital.

My heart pounded as my feet took over.

I followed up the stairs, down the corridor. He moved like someone with purpose. Not rushing. Just . . . certain.

He turned left into one of the conference rooms, and I hesitated—just for a breath—before stepping inside.

The room was filled with people.

Clara. Billy. Leanne. Jason. Diane. Mrs. Everly.

Even Michael from Brenner's Office Goods.

And there was Ben, standing near the cake, a goofy party hat perched on his head.

All smiling. All holding up a drink. All very pleased with themselves.

Above them hung a banner that read:

"To the Best Detective We Know—Happy Anniversary!"

Clara crossed the room. "Took you long enough, Watson," she whispered, eyes twinkling.

"So, my love. You orchestrated this mystery?" I bumped her shoulder with mine.

I needed a nudge. To get out of my rut, she would say. Turns out, I needed a case. A mystery. With cake.

Clara leaned close, lips near my ear. "O.B.," she whispered. "Other Ben." She grinned like it had been a private joke for years.

I stared at her.

"You hate being called Benjamin," she added.

I groaned. "You named the operation after my middle name?"

"Of course not," she said, eyes flicking toward our neighbor. "I named it after our other Ben."

It all came rushing back.

That same lopsided smile. The dimple.

His corny knock-knock jokes.

Ben raised his glass. "To Walter. The worst checker player in the world . . . and the best friend."

Clara knew—long before I did—that friendships are seeds.

Some just take a little longer to bloom.

I didn't say anything.

Just stood there, heart full, eyes stinging, surrounded by love and old ghosts brought back to life for one perfect moment.

Clara squeezed my hand.

I squeezed back.

Some mysteries are better than answers.

This one was both.

Knock-knock.

A Note from Walter

I never uncovered how many people were in on the mystery. Probably more than I'd guess. But no one spoiled it. That's the other kind of love—quiet patience so someone else can feel clever.

About the Author

Suzanne Parrott is a writer, illustrator, and publisher with more than four decades of experience in design and book production. As founder of First Steps Publishing, she has guided countless authors from manuscript to finished book, combining technical precision with a creative eye.

Her own work spans fiction, illustration, and educational resources, often blending humor, imagination, and thoughtful detail. With a background in both traditional and digital publishing, Parrott is dedicated to creating stories and designs that resonate, inspire, and last.

Together with Maren Eileen Sage and Anja Isdahl Elen, Parrott creates character-driven fiction that blends humor with reflection, inviting readers to linger in the small moments where memory and meaning cross paths.